STEPHEN ROBERT SUTTON

Understanding *Jodie*

Journal of a Teenage Goth

This publication contains the opinions and ideas of its author. It is intended to provide helpful and informative material on the subjects addressed in the publication. The author and publisher specifically disclaim all responsibility for any liability, loss or risk, personal or otherwise, which is incurred as a consequence, directly or indirectly, of the use and application of any of the contents of this book.

WORKBOOK PRESS LLC
187 E Warm Springs Rd,
Suite B285, Las Vegas, NV 89119, USA

Website: https://workbookpress.com/
Hotline: 1-888-818-4856
Email: admin@workbookpress.com

Ordering Information:
Quantity sales. Special discounts are available on quantity purchases by corporations, associations, and others. For details, contact the publisher at the address above.

ISBN-13:   978-1-956017-29-8 (Paperback Version)
                978-1-956017-30-4 (Digital Version)

REV. DATE: 11.08.2021

UNDERSTANDING JODIE

JODIE

:A JOURNAL OF A TEEN AGE GOTH

By: Mr. Stephen Robert Sutton

I AM --ME

POETRY THAT IDENTIFIES THE RIGHT TO BE AN INDIVIDUAL

Stamp Out Prejudice Hatred Intolerance Everywhere SOPHIE

In this age that we live in classed as the 21 century, we are categorised into groups of people that neatly form into a society of conformists. Anything beyond this is considered strange, odd or out of place, the individuals who are non conformists are cast aside and frowned upon like lepers. But what is worse than this is the abusive way they are treated for being different, verbal abuse by mocking and swearing at them and physical by attacking them in the street, often people in gangs do this. Some people are injured others killed just for being different, this can be initiated by the gangs wanting to bully people and in other cases it stems from their parents being racist, sexist, homophobic and passing their views down to their children.

For example take Sophie Lancaster a twenty year old victim of society

SOPHIE Stamp out Prejudice Hatred (and) Intolerance Everywhere

The murder of Sophie Lancaster occurred in England in August 2007. The victim and her boyfriend, Robert Maltby, were attacked by a group of teenage boys while walking through Stubbylee Park in Bacup, Rossendale, Lancashire, on 11 August 2007.[1] As a result of the severe head injuries Sophie sustained in the attack, she went into a coma from which she never regained consciousness, and died of her injuries thirteen days later. The police said the attack may have been linked to the couple wearing gothic fashion and being members the Goth subculture known as a hate crime.

Five teenage boys were later arrested and charged with murder. Two of them were convicted of murder and sentenced to life imprisonment. The other three were convicted and jailed for grievous bodily harm. A memorial fund was established in Lancaster's name, and numerous events have paid tribute to her locally, nationally and internationally. Plays, films, art and books have covered the issues surrounding the murder. (***Information obtained from Wikipedia 2021***)

This book is dedicated to the memory of her and all proceeds from the book will be going to the Sophie Lancaster foundation. The book consists of a number of poems and a story called 'Understanding Jodie' I hope you enjoy them and spread the word about my work and cause which is to treat everybody as an individual and respect their beliefs and feelings, help the weak ones and provide for those who cannot provide for themselves.

Jodie was based on at least three girls I knew who were friends, each of them were victims with hate crimes, the one was dyslexic, another dressed different and the other a lesbian each one never harmed anyone they just wanted to live their lives without fuss, one of these girls had one hand and often teased. The one that dressed differently was also asthmatic, the school gang found it funny when she mislaid her ventolin inhalor and was gasping for breath, often it was one of them that had hidden it. The dyslexic girl was teased because she couldn't spell and was clumsy due to dyspraxia, often tripping up, falling down stairs sometimes with assistance, one of the local gangs even beat one girl up in a frenzied attack. So in a sense Jodie was very real and the story although it was fictions, it was based on fact, I wrote understanding Jodie in the first person as if I am Jodie writing her journal I thought it may come across better. The character Jodie is forth right and opinionated; she is a lesbian and classes herself as an individual with her own style of dress and does not believe in conforming to society and its rules and regulations, or rather she is not a conformist. Jodie is classed as a free spirit with her own ideas, she hates bullies, she hates those who disrespect others and she dislikes antisocial behaviour. She is classed as a target for all those who find it difficult in accepting someone like her, the story is brief but to the point, I hope you enjoy it and understand the meaning behind it. This is Jodie's journal or diary called understanding Jodie.

S R SUTTON AUTHOR AND POET 2013

The poems come first in this book followed by Jodie's journal

ABOUT THE AUTHOR

I am S R Sutton author of fantasy horror novels and poetry. I have spent years of my life perfecting this art and feel passionate about many causes. It is my aim to demonstrate to the world exactly how I feel about society today living in Manchester. I haven't always lived here; I grew up in Lichfield Staffordshire got educated at Chadsmead infants and junior school and went on to Netherstowe, where I developed my gift as an artist and appreciation of poetry.

I was a care assistant for sixteen years before going into further education and going to Salford University graduating in 1999 and becoming a qualified general nurse. I entered education again at Manchester University as a student mental health nurse. My writing skills developed from writing essays and I was soon able to produce novels such as Cracked Porcelain, Understanding Jodie and the Harrington curse under various names such as Sarah Ruth Scott and Simon Robert Sinclair with the initials SRS. I continued to write poetry from 1988 to the present 2021, writing five books of poetry including Manchester and beyond poems from Manchester, Life (as we know it) Deep in thought, Out of the Jar and The Best of life, the worst of life. My children Gemma, Jeni, Mike and Dan say they are proud of me, I respond by saying I do my best, this is what I tell everyone to just do your best.

(I AM) ME BY STEPHEN SUTTON

I am me, I am myself
All alone on my shelf
I want be my own identity
I want to live life totally free

This is the person
This is who I am
I could be a black sheep
Or a fluffy lamb

But I am an individual
One of a kind
I know what I want
I know my own mind

So don't criticize me
Don't peck at my head
For I am not lazy
Waste life in my bed

I just want my freedom
To be left alone
Without hateful abuse
Please leave me on my own

S.O.P.H.I.E BY STEPHEN SUTTON

Stamp out prejudice hatred
And intolerance everywhere
Embrace individual thoughts
And show them you care

Provide meaning and purpose
To those all around
Just because you are different
You are still sound

In memory of Sophie
Her name will live on
In a place in our hearts
We are as one

We fight for the right
The right to be me
As a free person

For all to see

END ALL HATE CRIMES

The world is at war
With hate crimes it's clear
Gangs of all colours
That's how they appear

Asians and blacks
White people as well
Fight for supremacy
Living in hell

So sit for a moment
Give it some thought
Is it all worth?
The way that you fought

With hatred and contempt
For your fellow man
To hate all those people
Whoever you can

You hate their colour
The way that they speak
All those who are different
All those who are meek

So end all hate crimes
Let peace lead you on
Love those who are different
Live life as one

HORRORS OF WAR

The cry of hunger
The moaning of pain
For here we are starving
Once again

Our bodies are thin
We feel very weak
With no one to help us
The future is bleak

The tears that we shed
Are common to me
If you want to see poverty
Then just look at me

The bloody battle still rages
With explosions all around
There is screaming and shouting
A horrific sound

Caught in a war
That we didn't need
Stop all this fighting
You hear us plead

LET THE CANDLES BURN
by Stephen Robert Sutton

Let the candles burn through the night
Let it burn now ever so bright
Let it flicker away but never ever go out
May it remind me to never live without a doubt

Let the candles burn and remind me of the truth
Of you and me when we were in our youth
Light up all the room with candles for each year
And may we think of a time when we would shed no tear

While the candle burn I will have company
Light those candles so I can see
Burn away in my room tonight
And forever make it bright

Burning softly in the breeze
Flickering candles putting me at ease
Slowly they go out one by one
Now I know that we are one

The candles were my burning life
Now they are gone I shall take flight
So let the candles burn in heaven instead
And put my thoughts and dreams to bed

HATED CRIMES BY STEPHEN SUTTON

How can we justify hate for others?
When never even met
Do we remember being bullied?
So easy we forget

More hate crimes in the news
When will they end?
Do we call ourselves the guilty?
Never making friends

The victims lay before us
Kicked and in a state
Who is guilty for their beating?
Who do you even hate?

You tease the way they dress
You hate the way they speak
You hate the way they live their life
And when they turn the other cheek

Why can't you show them mercy?
Why can't this hatred end?
Why don't you just accept them?
And show them you're a friend

UNDERSTANDING JODIE
by Stephen Sutton

Jodie was a lovely girl
She wrote her journal well
She wrote about her teenage life
As if she lived in hell

Her sexuality was a problem
She never could understand
To live her life as a lesbian
Why can't people understand?

Understanding Jodie
Wasn't hard to do
Understanding all her problems
You haven't got a clue

Oh to be a Goth
Wearing all the gear
With make up on her face
Why do others fear?

It's me beneath this costume
I am really quite like you
But this is my identity
You could be like me too

Try to get to know me
My desires and my need
All you see is my suffering
And how I seem to bleed

Believe me I am no freak
No rocky horror too
I am not your enemy
No alien to you

ALL OR NOTHING

Put into life what you have got
Add in some more if you have a lot
Conjure ideas again and again
Keep on going tax your brain

Giving it your effort all your best
Put everything in and sod the rest
Give it your blood give it your soul
Give everything empty your bowl

Make all the effort to be a success
Don't hold nothing back or get in a mess
Follow your fortune follow your fame
Always remember be ahead of the game

Your talent is wasted while you are asleep
So use your time wisely life is not cheap
Be part of the stream flowing smoothly along
Be patient with yourself you can't go wrong
It's all or nothing people will say

NOBODY LISTENS
by Stephen Robert Sutton

Nobody listens
Nobody cares
Nobody wants to
Nobody dares

Frightened to speak
Left on the shelf
No one understands
My mental health

Vicious and spiteful
Echoes remain
No one is listening
To those insane

I speak of my illness
My problems in life
You cannot see madness
Not without strife

The darkness is present
The demons appear
You cannot see them
But believe me they're here

Nobody listens
To the words that I say
They think I am sane
But I muddle through the day

One day they will listen
And remember my name
Find my poor body
And say what a shame

Nobody listens
Nobody cares
Nobody wants to
Nobody dares

This poem is about mental illness and how
professionals fail to listen to patients

WHEN I FALL
by Stephen Robert Sutton

Who is going to catch me?
When I fall
Who is going to comfort me?
When I feel small

Are you going to find me?
When I am lost
Will you reimburse me?
For any cost

Are you going to forgive me?
When I do wrong
Are you going to sing me?
A comforting song

When I fall
Will you pick me up
Holding your hands
Like a plastic cup

Will you catch me?
When I fall
Will you make me feel
Ten feet tall

SILENT WORLD
by Stephen Robert Sutton

No one knows
The way I feel
But in my world
You know its real

The silent world
I live my days
Without a sound
These are my ways

To see mouths move
Without a sound
Cars and buses
Moving all around

The birds are singing
Dogs bark out loud
Living in my silent world
Is really profound

I miss such a lot
Not hearing at all
I can't hear the clock
Ticking on the wall

We take for granted
What we hear and see
But just for a time
Please think of me

DO YOU SEE ME
by Stephen Robert Sutton

Do you see me?
Do you care?
Am I invisible?
Just in the air

Do you see through me?
Like a ghost in the night
So do I scare you?
Fill you with fright

You walk right past me
Like I am not there
With no acknowledgement
Like you don't even care

You see only my fault
Like a lantern alight
Showing my madness
The goods not in sight

I look in a mirror
And I see my reflection
Is it really me?
Or just a deception

I want to scream
Just to be seen
Or trash everywhere
Just to be seen

Do you see me?
Could you just care?
Just speak to me
Make me aware

Another example of the feelings of a mental health patient

INJUSTICE
by Stephen Robert Sutton

What you see is in your head
The person you see alas is dead
You think what you do is right
But all it is, is a racist fight

Don't you see we have a right to live?
And it shows by the love we give
we pray to the same god above
And all we want is love

What we see is injustice I say
when all we want to do is pray
Pray for the weak and feeble in mind
I beg you don't be cruel but be kind

Don't judge a man by his skin
But look at the man within
He bleeds red blood like you and I
So don't make his family cry

At the injustice that you create
Or you surly deserve the same fate
One bad deed to end the day
By your reckless act, by your display

ME AND MY SELVES
by Stephen Robert Sutton

How do I start to explain?
About my life when I was sane
Was it real or was it not
To be honest I have almost forgot

About the trauma and the pain
And about the day I went insane
The brutal things that happened to me
I was once in captivity then set free

My mind was whole and now it's apart
Like the chambers of my heart
First I am Frank, and then I am John
How I wish I was only one

So many people in one head
Am I Alan or am I now Fred
One moment a boy then I am a man
Trying to reason as much as I can

My mind is so split I can't see the truth
Why was I abused in my youth?
These people protect me those in my head
The only time I am free is when I am in bed

FADED LIGHT

Like a faded light
You appeared to me
With a boastful grin
Fading into iniquity

But your sins will get you
In the end
Like meeting
A long lost friend

Like a fading light
You came to be
A subject for
Controversy

This fading light
Is going out
And provide such answers
For those in doubt

Your religion
Will never save the day
Your thoughts will
Just simply fade away

EQUALITY AND DIVERSITY

No matter what religion
You profess to be
Think of equality
And diversity

Treating each other
As they want to be
Is equality
And diversity

Each person is
Their own identity
From is you
And freedom is me

Race and gender
Is nobody's choice
You're born this way
So you must rejoice

No one should judge you
For the colour of your skin
Nor the sex that you are
Under that skin

Just because of the difference
You see
No one should mock you
Just let you be

DYSPRAXIA

(It's just the way I am)

I make such excuse for the way I perform
But I have been like this since I was born
With no sense of direction or lack of control
Or not achieving or reaching my goal

I correct my steps so I don't fall
People laugh and make me small
I cannot even catch a ball
And when I walk I am sure to fall

Some days are good some days I am bad
Sometimes I will curse sometimes I am glad
My brain tells me one thing my body says another
Why am I like this I must ask my mother

Which is my left hand, which is my right?
Should I go to school and end up in a fight?
My routine tends to vary according to my day
Should I concentrate no way I play
It just the way I am I tell myself
I wish I was an ornament sat on a shelf
Something to admire attractive and nice
But this is me with the luck of the dice
Or they accept you for you'll never change

The
Dollhouse Keeper's
Catastrophe

OUT OF THE JAR
MY BOOK OF POEMS
STEPHEN ROBERT SUTTON

BEING DIFFERENT

Walking and talking in your own style

Just being you and wearing a smile

Wearing the clothes that you want to wear

Living your life without a care

Just being different showing your worth

The only one of your kind walking this earth

Alone or with company you're not really fussed

Doing what you want that is a must

Just being different to those you're around

Just being there without making a sound

People love you or hate or find you strange
Or they accept you, for you'll never change

DEEP IN THOUGHT

By the expression on your face
Your mind is in another place
A place that is distant like the stars
For all I know it could be Mars

In the deepest cavities of your mind
Who will know what you will find
The deepest thoughts, hope and schemes
Solving puzzles or analyzing dreams

Searching for answers of mysteries today
Holding onto thoughts or visions this day
Even more riddles enter your head
That seem accumulate when your in your bed

LIFE IN A JAR

This is a prison of life's long pain
As for the meaning let me explain
People suffer from anxiety and fame
Some are blind, deaf and some are lame
Without all these things they would go very far
Until this time they must live in a jar

Fame restricts you from the freedom to move
Make plans for the future that they disapprove
A clear direct guided by fools around
Controlled like a robot without any sound
You live every day in a jar

A lost identity you don't know who you are

The title is ambiguous as you can see
But it expresses all things to me
Whether you are ill or just a star
Just remember you live in a jar
Who said your world is an oyster expressions like that
Must have been crazy or some sort of Pratt

THE CURSED

Spirits of the past do see
A curse on a family
Mirrors just to see through
Like a gateway they come for you

Snakes, spiders and creatures come
To menace you when the curse begun
Voices crying out in fear
Touching you when they are near

Swamps devour you when you wake
Waters drown you in a lake
Fire consumes you in this hour
Or poison to your lips so sour

Deadly is the curse at night
You wake up screaming with a fright
Who knows what terror lies within?
As the mirror reveals its mighty Sin

SCARS

Be who you want to be

Do what you want to do

Live how you want to live

It's up to you

Forget what you need to forget

It's all in the past

Live for the present

It's with you at last

The scars do remind you

Of your past life that has been

Some scars are hidden

They will never be seen

Plan for your future

trips far ahead

But don't dream about them

You can't reach them from your bed

DIARY OF A TEENAGE DRUG ADDICT

I wake up this morning
With my hair in a mess
I can't help it
Oh I couldn't care less

Yesterday was better
I don't know why
I feel dreadful
I just want to die

Just the other day
I had a dream
It was far out
I had to scream

A week a ago
I heard of a death
I have memories of her
It's all that's left

A single flower
Floats in a gutter
What a sad loss
Is all I can mutter

Cry after cry is all that I hear
From my hospital bed
Another mind is empty
Gone out of his head

Pink red and orange
Is all I can see
Won't someone help me
Please set me free

MANCHESTER PRIDE
by Stephen Robert Sutton

Experience the rainbow
And support them if you may
No matter what's your sexuality
Being straight or being gay

Join the large procession
Travelling down the street
Transsexuals and all kinds
People you must meet

Manchester pride is happening
All those that count today
Demonstrate their freedom
And their right to be a gay

They dress in many colours
Like a rainbow in the sky
Stand and cheer them onward
As they wave and pass you by

Canal Street is alive
It is a bustling place
The queens of Manchester
Never look out of place

So join the pride of Manchester
With their banners flying high
And the rainbows of this world
Will shine in the sky

MANCHESTER TALENT
by Stephen Robert Sutton

As I look around Manchester
What do I find?
So much talent
It blows my mind

Such gifted people
And that's the truth
So much talent
In all our youth

Artist, musicians, writers
So many to find
Some that are homeless
Many you will find

People of all ages
With promising skills
So much creativity
It gives me the chills

Look at this city
See what you have got
Many fine crafts
They have the lot

Manchester's heritage
The talents are rich
Look at their work
And what they accomplish

So just recognise them
Just take a glance
Let them show you their talent
Please give them a chance

MANCHESTER AIR

by Stephen Robert Sutton

Arise arise to the Manchester air
Feeling free without a care
Breath it in within your skin
Just as you did when life did begin

All the races all of your kind
All your thoughts are brought to mind
Colour and creed are as one
Under the moon and under the sun

You working class have a place
All equal under Manchester's race
All alive and all do share
This our own Manchester air

We work together united in peace at this time
Live for a cause and don't commit any crime
And just as real as the stars above
We live for each other giving one love

Arise arise to the Manchester air
Feeling free without a care
Breath it in within your skin
Just as you did when life did begin

MANCHESTER PRISON
by Stephen Robert Sutton

How odd me thinks
The strange bleak place
Where theives and rogues do go
To think of things of yesterday
Or strange ways if you must know

Manchester prison was once known
By its inmates and officers too
Strange ways was just the place
Where prisoners were welcomed to

A tower stood with a wachful guard
Watching a prisoner escape in plight
They watched him leave and knew for well
The police would cathch him later at night

The prison warden paced up and down
Keeping a watchful eye
The prisoners were clear what to do
As they stole the governors pie

What was best there for the rest
Than fifteen years or a five year stretch
Doing your porridge fulfilling the time
Doing your penance for doing the crime

PICTURE OF INNOCENCE

She has the face of an angel
With eyes that care
A wonderful girl
With dark flowing hair

Her look of innocence
Right there on her face
Such a nice girl
With elegance and grace

As pure as the driven snow
That settles on the ground
She sends a fine message
With love all around

She appears quite timid
Like a lamb or a deer
But that's part of her appeal
To others so near

She's the type you protect
To keep her from harm
This is why she is popular
She's so full of charm

This was a poem about Kyra featured on the front cover from an observation of mine as a nurse, from working with her as a carer.

UNITED IN GRIEF
by Stephen Rober Sutton

I remember thee
At the sadness of the day
I stand and pray
Where the flower lay

Where poeple come
Across the street not murmuring a sound
The quietness showing respect
Tragedy they found

The senseless murder of local folk
It's such a senseless crime
Blown away and left for dead
Cut off in their prime

But all of you from Manchester
Witness an even so brief
Mourning side by side
United in your grief

People come and help them
Helping those in need
By giving of themselves
With courage they succeed

A concert is arranged
Raising money to help the cause
Showing solidarity
And a reason to end terrorist wars

GENDER CRISES

Who am I?
I don't know
Am I female?
Or just for show

Am I a person?
Who thinks and walks
Or a man
Who just thinks and talks

Am I a person?
Who questions my thoughts
Alters my body
From all marks and warts

Am I so weak?
Or am I so strong
Is it a problem?
or am I so wrong

I watch my body
I see it change
Is this unusual
Or is it so strange

Who am I?
And what is my sex?
What is my gender?
And is it the best

I want some answers
Please let me know
Give me some guidance
Let my life flow

DIFFERENT AGAIN

by Stephen Robert Sutton

I am an individual
One of a kind
Just different
That's all you will find

I am my person
With my own kind of style
With a winning personality
And a happy smile

I live my life
In my own special way
Just living
For each and every day

I really don't care
What people may think
I have fun in life
And know how to drink

I am so in control
And know what I need
And when I get cut

UNDERSTANDING JODIE

JOURNAL OF A TEENAGER

S R SUTTON

INTRODUCTION

This is the story about a girl called Jodie Brown told in her own words, Jodie was like any other teenage girl except she suffered from a common learning disability known as dyslexia. Most people would associate this problem as not being able to read and write properly. However the problem does not end there, other contributing factors add to the misery of not understanding words. I refer to short-term memory problems and poor concentration, which lead to frustration and behavioural problems.

But Jodie not only had this problem to contend with but the fact that due to her change in hormones and the usual stages of changing from girl to womanhood, she was also confused over her gender. She found herself desiring women and being attracted to her own female teacher. Jodie was confused by her teenage life and no one else fully understood

Jodie, she was a misfit and felt alone.

Jodie lived in a nice house with her parents and two brothers, Tom aged sixteen and Gary aged ten. Jodie was thirteen at this time and considered to be more mature than Tom in some ways. But as Jodie began to develop she thought back to the awful schooling that she had being bullied and began to rebel. She joined self-defence classes and became exceptionally good at kickboxing, however although she was good she never used it against anyone else. She was at school until she reached sixteen, then left and got a job in the retail trade.

But this was just the beginning of Jodie's rebellious teenage years, a Halloween party at school led to Jodie becoming a Goth and joining a rather savoury bunch of hooligans led by a man called by his friends Snake. Her time with this gang led her into all kinds of trouble until she finally found herself in prison experiencing an even rougher existence.

UNDERSTANDING JODIE   BY S R SUTTON
WRITTEN IN 2013 TAKEN FROM JODIE'S JOURNAL

INDEX

UNDERSTANDING JODIE
JOURNAL OF A TEENAGER

I am Jodie Brown and this is my journal read it at your peril, I am no angel I am also no fool by the time you read the end of this I will no doubt be in prison but who really cares. No one will shed a tear for me, as I fight life's burocracy single handed as Boudicea or Joan of Arc god bless her. Isn't life all about stamping out prejudice hatred and intolerance everywhere? Well the world needs to know this and have a good shake up before more victims end up like me or those who die trying to be themselves, read on.

SCHOOL BULLYING

It was just another winter's morning, as a blanket of snow lay thick on the ground. I suppose that I would be regarded as a typical thirteen-year-old girl wearing my school uniform with pride and carrying my school bag on my back. I suppose you would consider me pretty with my tanned skin, perfect teeth and large hazel eyes. I am slim and conscious of my weight never eating at regular times with a highly active lifestyle that burns my calories like a girl on fire, my god what a metabolism. I always put my hair into a pony tail, I suppose the colour is alright two tone brown, but no doubt when I am older I could be a blonde like my mother. Although I don't want to act like the snobby bitch god bless her, not me I am Jodie the individual still seeking my identity and that's hard on it's own let me tell you. I am Jodie Brown the individual with my own mind and my own thoughts, everyone else can do one.

My parents, well what can I say we live in a nice house, both my parents work so we look after ourselves most of the time. My younger brother Gary needs watching though, he is so naughty at times. My older brother Tom who is sixteen takes care of us both and walks Gary to school. I am old enough to make my own way to school, although the bullies are always there to ruin my day. I wonder what it will be today stealing my clothes from the changing room, flicking a towel at my Derry air or ruining my artwork. Maybe their simple minds will conjure up a new way of making my life a misery but that's what it's like at school so I suck it up.

On my way to school I enjoy walking down the avenue; I walk through the trees and gaze up at the long thin branches imagining I am in some enchanted Forrest in a fantasy world. I can admire the snow on the trees and feel the breeze blowing gently on my face. It is blowing a spray of snow down like flower being sieved onto a table; I wish I had my paints right now so that I could paint this picture. Art is my favourite subject at school I spend so much time in that classroom, I feel that I can escape from life in my pictures. I can create my own fantasy and dictate who does what and be a heroine with admirers all around me, I can see myself as Robin Hood or some other hero of the past.

As I left the avenue I continued to walk to school my dreams were suddenly shattered by the impact of a snowball to my head, then another to my back. The school bullies throwing snowballs at me one after the other surrounded me. I let out a scream that must have sounded worse than any horror movie; it was that loud penetrating the school building, it was almost blood curdling. Okay not that bad but enough to fetch the teachers out and stop the bullies in their tracks.

"Right Johnson, Dawson and Julie inside now" It was the booming voice of Mr Gilbert the maths teacher.

He was enough to scare anyone with his tall and broad physique, he was an ex boxer and one teacher that you would never answer back to. He watches each of them go inside and gave them a look of disgust for being bullies. Yeah right, as if that's going to change their attitude school career as bullies, they just get worse and attack you again later I know the fucking pattern. A girl was once beaten to death just for being different, the bastards got caught eventually but only when she was beaten so badly she died, another lad was kicked in the head and never recovered he is a cabbage.

The teacher turned and then he looked at me, a girl that was wet and shivering with cold, suddenly his facial expression changed from annoyance to sympathy as he spoke to me in a gentle voice

"You had better go inside and get dry girl, Mrs Cooper will help you"

This was like music to my ears the teacher that I drooled over was going to dry my hair and help me to change. My god could life get any better I had the worlds most beautiful woman as my teacher. Mrs Cooper led me into a room in the gym and began drying my hair as luck would have it she was wearing a white blouse that had a few buttons open. I could clearly see part of her breasts wobbling as she was vigorously rubbing at my hair. I was in ecstasy the whole time until she turned me round to dry the back; even then her knees were rubbing against my buttocks. The whole experience was very brief but enough to affect me physically.

I rejoined the class and sat through geography, but instead of studying the contours of land I was back with Mrs Cooper studying the contours of her body. This clearly questioned my sexuality, if I fancied the female teacher like this then was I a raving lesbian or maybe I was bi sexual?. I never thought of it before I was evidently growing up and noticing the human form. Sex classes were no help discussing reproduction and nothing to do with gender types, comparing masculinity and femininity as a way of spotting the difference between male and female.

The best part of geography was the school bell for the end of period; I have never seen a class empty as quickly as Miss Hammonds. She had to be the world's most boring person she could cause the entire class to go to sleep in seconds with her droning voice and she doesn't stop for breath. I have actually seen her turn blue before she began to breathe normally; what's more if she did collapse with her weight she could crush you instantly into mush. But god bless her she made the effort top marks for trying with the ignorant rabble in the classroom mainly the boys who were complete tossers.

I entered the toilets and as usual the female bullies were stood talking about boys and who would get a date first. I entered one of the cubicles and was suddenly drowned with water from the girls using plastic cups one after another. How I wished that they would find something original to do, the predictability of water being thrown over me I should carry an umbrella with me everywhere I go. I could clearly hear their silly giggling thinking how entertaining, how original and how pathetic.

Again I was thinking about that blonde twenty five year old teacher Mrs Cooper, I am going to date her definitely and she will take me back to her place and show me a good time. We would have Milkshake and chicken burgers with extra mayonnaise licking it off with her tongue. At that moment my fantasy ended with the banging of the door and a loud voice.

"Jodie Brown hurry up your late for English" the voice said
Wow, somebody knows my name top marks and please tell the rest of the school, meanwhile back to reality, the boredom of school through my brown eyes.

English was a lesson that I attend but never like, it's so hard to understand and I always end up daydreaming. I can't concentrate and get into so much trouble with the teachers. I spend most of my school life in front of the headmaster listening to his lectures on if he lived his life again he would be a brain surgeon or dentist, honestly I would sooner be punished by having the Cain by Mrs boring Hammond. God bless the old dears bloomers I bet she hasn't had a man since the turn of the century. She is busy fighting off the cob webs sad old cow, from no mans land, she is also a secret drinker, or so they say likes the old tot of sherry or gin, I wondered why she wobbled and zig zagged along the corridor like a pregnant duck.

As I sat in the English class one, my god, I was given a book to read by another dyslexic William Shakespeare. Romeo and Juliet honestly why couldn't it be called Juliet and Juliet at least I could try to read it. Juliet flashes her tits over the balcony and Juliet two (meaning me) tries to climb up and grope her lesbian style. I would like to know what thee and thou is all about is it teenage slang for thou can't climb because I hast a gammy leg. Can't someone translate this crap into readable English, sorry mate you lost me on verse one, I read a line and wanted to top myself. I can't sit through an hour of this, I must think of a plan of escape. Perhaps the vomit routine might do it although my stomach is empty, perhaps a migraine, no I did that yesterday. Well here goes under the table fingers down the throat and result all over the desk and one of the bitches that threw water over me. Take that super bitch in your hair and on your cloths, you will defo stink later, she responded by standing up quick and shouting, all the class laughed and I climbed to the top of the popularity pole for all of five seconds.

The teacher soon got me outside and I was back in the cubical calling Alf and Bert being sick down the loo. I soon recovered and sat thinking of Mrs Cooper once more. I must confess I did enjoy her classes even though she taught history I could imagine we were in the Napoleonic wars together or in Tudor times. I washed my face and looked at myself in the mirror wondering what I would look like at the age of thirty. Older and wiser with a different hair style and image without being terrified by the school bell knowing it was for class or break time. I would love to walk down the corridors without fear of being bullied by other students.

I used to play sports like tennis, basketball or hockey but I had problems in the shower or changing rooms because of other girls. They would steal my clothes or slap me, or push me against a cold locker. I have always been bullied and I have to say no one has ever been able to understand me. Understanding Jodie must be a contest and the winner gets to go to Disney for three weeks, well at least I understand me, I think.

I am cursed with a duff brain and a boring personality that's my lot in life, I have no real friends, parents that don't care and teachers I don't understand. But life goes droning on like Mrs Hammond god bless the old trout. I suppose some people would say that I am being too hard on myself but if you are criticised too much you believe in your own mind that you are no good. If I were to describe my life at thirteen I would say crap, I can draw, paint and do incredible things with clay but it ends there.

It was at this point that I considered that's enough, I have been the subject of ridicule bullied beyond belief and so I took up martial arts. My favourite was kickboxing, my instructor said that I was champion material and he wanted me to go into contests. I have to say for a man he was nice and so kind, I built up mental and physical strength through him teaching me. He taught me how to control my emotions and channel it into my boxing, he demonstrated how to get rid of pent up frustration but then he never met Mrs Cooper. What a challenge that would be even for him if she joined his class he would have a permanent erection to deal with. God bless Mr George saveloy Sidwell so called because of his big sausage penis. If Mrs Cooper was in his class there would be no boxing only pole vaulting.

In cookery class we had a Mrs Totter with the most enormous arse ever, whenever she bent down to take something out of the oven we had a total eclipse of the sun or the moon shining. My god could she cook, she was a wonder with her pastry and roast chicken, she reminded me of a turkey with her fat arse waggling. Her chins dangled nicely down and her hair stuck up in the air, short red and sticky. I managed to bake cookies and cakes

Thinking about my family I must mention the formal dinners that my dear parents were so proud of, they used to invite their well to do friends to these functions. Some of them were so weird and had horrendous table manners, my god they were awful. People like Janet and Brian, Janet would slurp her soup and Brian chewed his food like a camel. His mouth went into the most amazing contortions and I swear I could see every item of food that he consumed over dinner in his mouth. Janet kept tooting like a Kangaroo with turrets, it was about as entertaining as watching an angry pussy spot burst. We were told to watch our manners and sit up at the table, bleeding hypocrites, why should we innocent creatures be subject to this torture every month. Its child cruelty of the highest order and not for the faint hearted, it needs a government health warning. Parent's guests are bad for your health, especially when they embarrass you with stupid remarks about how you look like this relative or that. Or pointing out your skin condition or the way you wear your hair it's simply oh my god how you can even comment you sag sacks. I think my parents must have chosen their friends from a circus full of freaks.

And as for parties well all of them appeared in one room like they had been kidnapped and brought to the house. My god all of them in one room, how can they be so cruel as to put us through that. I thought even the Spanish inquisition wasn't as bad as this; it's so amazing what they put us children through. One couple were small in stature and I remember my parents lecturing us on being careful what we said. Tact and diplomacy were the key words in this case. But isn't it the case that, the more you try to avoid saying anything the more you slip up. My father asked them if they wanted a short meaning a drink of wine or something, I nearly died and this was followed by similar references to their stature. None of these remarks were meant to offend them, but they inevitably did as they came at them like a verbal machine gun. But despite the remarks they continued visiting my parents as if they love to be insulted, my god I can imagine them saying I don't come here to be insulted and my father replying well where do you usually go? But my parents were really sociable and kind, they were popular with many people. I really don't blame them for the way I turned out; after all I was a raving teenager who was out to avenge the world for my horrendous school days.

REACHING PUBERTY

I have already discussed my desire for women and the closer that I got to puberty the worse it got. I did concentrate in the classes on sexual development but again nothing mentioned about Lesbianism so that was balls. Oh but did the lecturer go on about periods like it was the only thing in life that mattered. Describing the time of the month (or the monthly cycle) as the breaking away of the uterus wall and a rush of blood flowing out, or something like that. Why didn't she say it would happen in English class at 10.00am when I was sat relaxed and not wearing a sanitary pad, what a soft bitch?
I was so embarrassed and wanted the ground to open and swallow me up. I wonder how many women have had accidents like that, god I nearly bled to death right there and even the boys nearly fainted it was like a massacre. My god you would think I could have had some sort of warning, for instance a bell ringing from down below or buzzer. Look out flood coming and it's blood, I felt like my incontinent granny on a bad day, how awful too bad this didn't happen to the boys through their back passage, here comes sympathy.

Apart from the near death experience I was shocked by how quick by breasts developed from tiny hills to mountains and not to mention the pubic hair, which grew like a thorn bush, both armpits were also blessed with the bush. Suddenly I was a woman its official the evidence was visible and even my body shape had altered into more curvy hips. Naturally this didn't happen overnight but over a few years I was now reaching sixteen and looking back at my early teens wondering how I survived. The bullying continued but the gangs were targeting new blood I was left to the hard-core bullies who concentrated their energies on the strong survivors.

The bullies reminded me of my embarrassing period in the English class by finding a sanitary towel and covering it with tomato sauce leaving it in my desk draw. Then making me know that it was there with subtle hints and innuendos very mature of them. I remember standing naked looking at my new body in a full-length mirror at my front and then the back. I touched my breasts and rubbed my nipple until they went hard, it was like someone had given me a new toy to play with. Here is your new body Jodie. I was also fascinated with my pussy, it was a new discovery and exciting to touch, I soon mastered the art of masturbation and enjoyed this immensely. I used to watch my fellow pupils in the shower and wonder what they would look like when they developed fully. I watched Television and movies and got turned on by the latest celebrities, women of course, my god they were gorgeous. I was entering a new world and loving it, all I desired was here before me and Mrs Cooper was at the top of my list. A sex goddess in my own classroom, my god if I have not said before, I loved that lady and wanted her for my own. I was mature now that I had reached puberty so I could effectively be with her and we could have a thing going, my god dream on Jodie.

The puberty thing led its natural course to self-discovery as my friends and I shared over an ice cool milk shake and sweet doughnut. We were in a local cafe enjoying each other's company when the subject of sex, boys and girls came up. I had already indicated my desire for women and so Rachel asked me about my interests in the female form, she was as subtle as a flying mallet asking me the question 'Are you gay?'

"Well what do you think" I replied sharply

"Oh shit Jodie I didn't know" Rachel replied embarrassed on hearing the answer.

"My god Rachel you must have known" I said staring her right in the face.

"No honestly I didn't" Rachel said innocently.

"But all the things I said before, you must have picked up clues" I said trying to explain.

"So how long have you known Jodie?" Rachel continued

"Since my body started changing I suppose" I said looking down onto my and pointing to my breasts.

SELF DISCOVERY

I already knew about my sexuality and gender orientation, I was a female but had no interest in males, the male form to me was revolting and about attractive as cow shit. I wanted to experience sex with men just to prove the point. So I arranged to date a boy from school who I knew had a little experience with women in others words a male slag. John Green was anything but green he was said to be the hottest lover in school and I was the one to have sex with him convince him that I loved him and dump him. I was called the black widow spider because a black widow spider makes love with the male then will destroy him. I was right of course the most boring experience of my life and not worth returning to in a hurry. I don't rock to cock no way; I would rather have a donut with jam or cream. Of course I never really let on that I was gay just thrived on humiliating poor John, he became a right wanker of course. So that was me, my identity Jodie the dyslexic lesbian.

My first female sexual experience was with a girl called Katie Barnes god bless her, we made out in the drama room. The front door was locked and we crept into the room via the stage from the main hallway. We had not intended to make love as we were just exploring looking for costumes to wear for a school production later that year. Katie was very forward and very sexually active while I was still a little bud waiting to flower. I had stripped off to change into another costume, she was helping me get ready and began touching me making out she was doing it by accident when in reality she wanted to fondle my breasts. Yes I had developed and she was amazed at the size of my boobs, she was staring at me and asked me if I had ever kissed a woman. I replied no and watched her lick her lips like she had been eating a doughnut and was trying to lick away the excess jam and sugar from her lips. I must confess this was turning me on, but I was nervous and shy this was a new experience for me.

She moved forward and began to kiss me, her tongue entered my mouth and seemed to curl around mine it felt very wet, but nice wet and warm. I felt my entire body tingle and wanted more, she was certainly a dominant girl and I was so submissive. I let her take control and she began to kiss my neck and licked at it like a lioness making noises like purring. I was beginning to relax succumbing to her desire and being aware that she was seducing me. I felt her undo my bra and my breasts lay naked so that she was able to caress them, my nipples hardened as she touched them. We then lay down on the wooden floor and I felt my body react as she continued to make love to me. My rose began to bloom and the morning due appeared on the rose petals in a way I never experienced before. Not even John Green was able to make my body throb as she did, as I reach a wonderful and record breaking orgasm. I was in total ecstasy my only regret was that this experience wasn't with Mrs Cooper.

After this event we regularly went to the same place and enjoyed lesbian sex in the same way. I knew then that I never ever wanted to be straight and that my future would be with women not men. I had always desired women but had never dipped my cherry before and so hadn't experienced the wonders of same sex relationships. My future was equally as colourful but that another story and there is much more to tell about my rebellious life. I regret few things in my life and I must say we all make love differently that's what makes a colourful world.

My schooling continued with very little problems I struggled through my classes due to dyslexia, no one helped of course. My parents despaired at my school reports and questioned me about my behaviour. I had a attitude but didn't care because I got no support and was expected to cope with subjects despite my disability. My teachers concentrated on the bright pupils and fuck the rest, so I continued in my own sweet way. My god no one understands Jodie or ever will, I am just crap under their shoes and people don't give a fuck about me. Jodie the no nobody and Jodie the troublemaker forget my achievements in art or my amazing ideas. I was fed up of existing in a classroom full of time wasters and rebels and I wanted to fit in somewhere. I had wondered what it must be like being in a gang and not being picked on as an individual, I would be protected for once and not expected to defend myself. I would belong to a group of people and share their life style and learn new things from them.

Camp trips had to be the highlight of my schooling, whoever created the idea of camping I could kiss them. Each year pupils would be chosen for their academic achievements or good behaviour in class, guess which category I went under. Well it was the good behaviour of course; at least it was for the duration of the year when I might be chosen. We travelled on the coach and I sat next to my friend Rachel as usual, my dishy best mate. We had just set off when I heard the sound of someone vomiting, my god the smell was revolting, I could not enjoy my small bar of chocolate with someone having a hughy behind me. The moment was lost and I had let my chocolate melt through my fingers as I waited for her to stop.

On the journey to the camp all I could think of was Rachel's body especially her legs, I thought to myself my god how can such a lovely body be wasted on a straight girl. I wish she was gay and then I could have my wicked way with her in our tent. At this moment I altered my thoughts to the countryside at the roving hills and sparkling lake scenes so shapely just like Rachel, my god I am at it again with my perverse thoughts. Shit I hope the camp trip does not affect me, I must stay focused on something else or I am going to regret what I could potentially do. The fact that I am gay doesn't matter but to hit on my best friend my god that would be the cardinal sin.

We arrived on camp fairly late considering both the teachers and the driver professed to know the way. They had a navigation system and a map so how did they go wrong, oh don't tell me males created both of them and males were trying to understand them. Who is sexist my god it's a wonder we ever got there, the word dick head springs to mind. Never the less we made it in one piece, then came the putting up of the tents in the dark and the cussing and swearing that went on was worse than going down a mineshaft or entering a factory. It was all shit, fuck and bollocks and that was the clean stuff, my god I have never heard so much foreign language even in France. Once the tents were up (helped by a few torches of course) we were all told to assemble outside the tents while we were allocated our tents. Of course we got the usual lecture about behaving and sticking to the school rules, this meant no smoking, drinking, swearing, stealing and doing anything to upset the other pupils or teachers. Yeah like that's going to happen, like we will not obey any of their crappy rules, we are here to have fun in life.

Nobody mentioned sex I wonder why, is it because Mr Harvey fancied the knickers off Mrs Lewis from science, Old Harvey was one of the geography teachers who wanted to explore most female teachers contours and knock them off their equator. He was just a saucy bastard who had a permanent volcano in his trousers; you could tell when he had an erection when he walked sideways. Talk about tent pole he could jack up a car with that mother, I pity Mrs Lewis my god she was in for a challenge. Talk about the cave of wonders, he would need a good light to go potholing there.

It was actually day two when he got his wicked end away, How gullible does he think we are, my god he went into the Mrs Lewis's tent just after midnight, Rachel and myself stayed awake to hear her enter his tent and then we crept up and fastened the tent flaps with safety pins, then by five O'clock we heard her struggling to get out. I must say they must think we are deaf as they give it throttle in the sack, moaning and groaning do they think we are so daft that we think it's the wildlife. And what would their respective partners think of them acting this way on camp. The following nights he was flapping her tent flaps and this time he put his foot in a cow pat, god the smell followed him everywhere for days. Funnily enough Mrs Lewis didn't visit him for days afterwards. She stuck to her own tent flaps, the crazy cow acting all innocent throughout the rest of the trip.

On camp we got involved with competitive sports such as tennis, rounders and tug of war. Here came my big moment as I played rounders as a dyspraxic student. I couldn't catch a cold even worse a ball, for me to be fielding was a complete wonder and disaster in one. I stood there watching the play and then low and behold my moment came, as the ball flew in the air and descended right above me. I cupped my hands and it was like slow motion as the ball landed right in the palm of my hands. Glory, I had actually caught the fucking ball, my god me actually catching the ball and everyone applauded me. I was living the moment right here, right now like the moon landing.
Well I have a new name for Mrs Lewis; I shall call her either Mrs Scabby knickers or sticky knickers which ever suits her most. She had certainly seen action in her merry little life as she made her way through the male teachers, I am truly grateful that she don't like woman as well. The anorexic nymphomaniac would have a field day with everyone, well she is different and to be admired for that, her own person or an individual.

The remainder of the camp trip was like carry on camping without the carry on crew. The showers were cubicles with holes in the walls with the male shower rooms next door, oh now where have I seen that before, yes in a scene from carry on camping with Sid James looking through the hole at naked women like Barbara Windsor. But I was prepared with towels and such to cover the holes or a good deodorant to sting the eyes. No purvey men were seeing my naked body or female bits.

Mr Lawrence the religious teacher was with us on the camping trip, he joined us for spiritual guidance. To be perfectly frank I would have preferred a nun with a dirty habit or even the pope in drag. Mr Lawrence was a soft tit, who hated lesbians and thought that it was a sin for the same sex people cohabitate and have sexual intercourse together,. I considered him to be lost up his own rectum and suggested that he read the beano instead of the bible. A child's comic would provide him with more insight than what he referred to as god's word, bless the dozy bullock. I was often criticized by Christians and Muslims alike who clearly did not understand anything about Lesbianism, what about reproduction they asked? "Fuck that, what about my own state of mind" I replied.

The only other things I remember from camp were the flatulence and the horrendous food leading up to this condition. Some of the pupils could strike up a band with the farting, it's a wonder that we didn't have explosions all over the camp when they sat by the camp fires to sing. We had burnt offerings almost every night which was said to be a barbecue, I am sure that the Australians didn't introduce this sort of barbecue to England. The songs were boring too what the hell is a ging gang goolie or whatever they were singing was it a testicle that hung funny.

So we went to bed and during the night we heard the sound of the wind howling through the trees and the odd bang. It sometimes sounded like whistling and explosions. My god we are under attack from al-Qaeda or some other terrorist air raid, maybe even the Russians. Rachel jumped into my bed and I must confess I was glad she did, speaking from a completely selfish point of view. I could feel her trembling body close to mine and I swear she had wet herself with fear, but I wasn't prepared to let her go as I was comforting her. She was convinced that we were under attack and were sure to die, imagine ending our lives here and not even experiencing full on snogging. It was at this point that we heard thunder followed by a heavy rain pour as the heavens really opened thrashing at the tent. Rachel and I sighed with relief and fell off to sleep in each other's arms, by the morning I had turned my back to Rachel and she had clung to my back. I could feel Rachel's breathe on the back and my god I felt horny, I had turned so not to get so turned on by her body. She suddenly woke up and climbed across me to look outside the tent.

"Come and look at this" she invited me to look outside.
"My god" I exclaimed as I looked around the camp only to notice that all the tents but ours had blown over.

It looked a complete mess with loads of tent poles and canvases everywhere, but where were the pupils and teachers?

We later discovered that they had all slept in an ex army billet that we would have used had we not gone camping. We had a good mountain tent and so we were comfortable, safe and dry, unlike our poor unfortunate friends. I have to confess to feeling exhilarated for more reasons than none, after all some of these were bullies from school. This is what I consider rough justice and as the religious teacher Mr Lawrence would say god moves in mysterious ways. I call it rough justice although some of the teachers and pupils were not so bad.

Moving sweetly on in a fashion that I had become accustomed to I began to really get annoyed with the bullies. I was always getting in trouble with other girls or teachers although I earned respect when I dumped John. I was termed as lazy, thick and no good so much that I was beginning to believe it myself. But what everyone didn't believe was that I wanted to get on in school and be academic but my dyslexia was holding me back.

Mrs Cooper helped me but one day I was given the news that she had tragically died in a road traffic accident. I was in shock I couldn't eat, drink or sleep my world was turned upside down.

I headed for the toilets and threw my ring up, suddenly the bowl became huge and my head seemed small inside it. I clung hold of the sides and felt dizzy. At that moment I heard a voice outside taunting me challenging me to a fight, we were near the gymnasium and I thought this was it my chance to finish the bullying.

Donna welsh was built like a sumo wrestler big, mean and ugly with only one brain cell floating in her head. I could hear the bitch shouting abuse at me and banging at the cubicle door.

"Hey black widow come out here and get laid lesbian bitch" Donna shouted loudly in a mean menacing voice.
I opened the door and stared her in the eyes; her pig like eyes looked back at me with pure hate written across her expression.

We both walked into the gym and two other women each accompanied her holding a bat as a weapon.

"I hear you don't like me bitch" Donna said angrily

"I never said that" I replied confused

"Are you fucking calling me a liar" Donna continued

"No" I made it clear I wanted no trouble "I want no trouble"
"What's that noise, I hear a mouse squeaking" Donna looked back at

her friends for support.

"Me too" said one of the gang

"Don't tread on the mouse girls" Donna said sarcastically

"I'm no mouse" I replied bravely or stupidly I suppose
"Sorry you squeaked girl, fuck she squeaked" Donna suddenly hit me in the stomach with her bat.

I fell to the ground holding my stomach one of the women went to hit me with her bat when Donna stopped her

"This bitch is mine" Donna said watching me trying to get up

"I said I don't want trouble" I told them again remembering the self control that my instructor taught me.

Again Donna hit me this time in the ribs, this time I fell backwards but remained standing as she thumped me in the nose.

I felt the blood trickle down and onto the floor and knew by now I had to defend myself. Donna rushed forward to attack again this time I swerved to one side and she hit the wall with the force of her body. I quickly turned and kicked her in the small of her back and she fell like a sack of potatoes. One of the other women raced to her defence and was immediately knocked to the ground with a kick to the throat. The other woman tried a pathetic punch, which didn't even connect, and I simply kicked her legs from under her and delivered a blow to her stomach.

Donna tried to get up but I thumped her repeatedly on the face and drop kicked her in the chest and she rapidly returned to the ground.

At that point the teacher came in clapping slowly

"Oh very good Jodie Brown, excellent for your school record" the teacher went on "So what do you do for an encore, break bones?"

I was so surprised at her attitude considering I was defending myself "But miss I was ganged up on they were trying to beat me up" I said knowing that I was on to a loser.

"Looks like it Jodie, I think you beat them up" She said almost smiling I really think she thought I was in the right but could not admit it.
At this point my parents were called into school and the facts were so twisted not even a judge would be able to fathom out the truth. My parents were certainly shocked at my behaviour but then they didn't quite understand my dyslexia or in fact why they had me in the first place from what I could see both sat in the office not saying a word. Neither mother or father gave me eye contact, I was just listening to the whole circus wondering why I bothered defending myself in the first place.

The head of school gave a nice speech about self-control and how I apparently beat up three girls and used kickboxing to do this. The only one who actually believed me was George my instructor; he was not surprised at the story as I related it to him, according to George self defence can be a case of you defending yourself but the attackers injuring themselves through their own efforts to hurt you. But unfortunately that didn't help this situation and my school record.

"I have something to say" I announced proudly

Everyone looked at me as if I had two heads, not one person actually cared what I thought, but I continued anyway.

"When I was seven and being bullied who helped me and as the years went on did I get help with dyslexia, no I didn't, and then I came to this poxy school and was I bullied again yes I was and was I helped, no I wasn't, so the day I fight back its all sympathy to the other poor girls but me I get punished. My god where's the justice in that?" After I given my elaborate speech for justice the room was silent I felt that I had given my all and that everyone would sympathize or even empathize but nothing. It was as if I had simply farted and not apologised for my actions, wasted gas from the ass a pointless exercise for me.

However I did gain the respect of the school pupils after this day, I was conscious of the golden rule of not getting the other girls in trouble by telling the head teacher about their antics. Donna never approached me again and wanted me to join her gang, naturally I refused that treat and continued with my artwork without any further problems. I realised bullies just needed to know that they were not going to get away with hurting other pupils and that was good enough reason to punch the lights out of the bullies. The secret was to find the leader of a gang or ringleader and beat them up first, like skittles find the strongest and hit that and watch the others fall. Simple logic that even the dumbest person could work out, I was considered thick, but I proved that I was knowledgeable at times.

I hated being called out of class to the special lesson for dyslexia or other learning difficulties. It was quite obvious where we were going, when the special needs teacher blurted it out in class. My god, why didn't she just blow a trumpet and announce it properly like,
"Jodie, can you please come to your dyslexic class!" Honestly how discrete is that and my form teacher didn't help as she pointed me out so that all the other pupils would see me. My god I wanted to die on the spot or hope the ground would open up and swallow me whole. My entire school days were embarrassing for one reason or another, poor Jodie the one no one understood or the dyslexic lesbian.

OH TO BE A GOTH

The next phase in my life happened by accident as I pointed out I never wanted to be in any gang, I never agreed to gangs or the problems that went along with them. Usually a gang hanging around a street corner meant trouble and could look menacing for others.

At first it was like experimenting with make up, mainly black, with a subtle application of rouge to give a pale effect to the skin which also covered up the present acne problem. Then the eye liner and mascara with a hint of purple or blue on the eye lids and surrounding area. With black eye brows and black lip stick, I had already dyed my hair black and dressed in black with a black necklace and black nail varnish I was almost ready for the schools Halloween party.

I wore a black skirt and black tights with stylish boots to match and a black-laced blouse; looking back I was a dead ringer for Morticia from the Adams family. Such a scary sight to behold but fitting for a Halloween party, which was arranged by the school for a get together of students, teachers and parents. It was well organised I must admit but guess who's parents didn't attend? Yes surprise mine god bless them.

I reached the school hall and noticed quite a few people dressed for the occasion. It was most impressive inside like a horror movie film set such as Van Helsing with a long buffet like Harry Potter's Hogwarts School. It was a good turn out the hall was packed with witches, devils and vampires all feasting. But something was wrong not all the people fitted in seemingly slightly out of place, particularly one gentleman who stood out with his strange top hat and long black coat. He even acted oddly as he walks around with a blonde woman who seemed to frown at everyone.

He finally stood in front of me and eyed me up and down, then looked at his companion.

"Marsha my dear I think we have found a Goth" He said confidently Marsha didn't seem impressed gazing at me and then brushing her blonde hair back with her hand. She was dressed very much like me but had some sort of flower in her hair.

"Well be polite and say hello" He insisted

"Hello" She said reluctantly

"My name is snake, and who might you be?" Snake asked

I looked at his rather long nose and narrow face, I remember thinking he was skinny enough to be a snake, long and thin.

"I am Jodie" I said hesitantly

"But people call you black widow" He said looking at Donna across the hallway.

"I have been known as the black widow for certain reasons" I smiled at him because I knew what he was referring to.

"Poor Johnny got his tail cut off with you the spider who eats his lover after making love, I like it". Snake smiled cunningly.

I suppose Snake could come across creepy at first, but he had a lovable side to him. He had a dry sense of humour and loved the mystical side of life; he was very much into Gothic art and music.

As for Marsha she was very much in love with Snake and was so jealous of me, she detected an attraction between Snake and myself I was merely fascinated by him but he was attracted to me sexually. Marsha refused to speak to me from this day forward; she also had a cruel streak in her and would often use it to push away possible admirers of Snake.

Snake was almost like a Messiah, people often followed him and would do anything he said, they latched on to his every word and believed that he possessed magical powers. His disciples were all around him most of the time I met them later when I visited their hang out as he called it.

It was a old disused church or at least the ruins which lay close to the city.

I left the party with Snake, Marsha and a strange little man called shady he was called this because he liked to walk in shaded areas and he was so quiet. Once in the ruins I met Juicy Lucy a blonde bimbo who was always giggling Mash a fat boy who loved mash potatoes, Clay who was a big hard man who never smiled. Fudge was a fat girl who was always eating, Drab was a girl who dressed more plainly and came out with boring things. The rest were not even mentionable and easily forgotten, all followed Snake and listened to his words of wisdom.

All I heard initially was Goth music being played constantly and the odd smell of cat piss which indicated someone was on the wacky backy or cannabis. Snake approached me after attending the church a few nights

"If you're with us you need to prove it" He looked serious

"What do you mean" I asked not knowing what to expect

"Oh like an initiation into our gang" He replied looking at the others

"What do I do?" I said worried to death that he might get me to eat a live toad or sacrifice a lamb.

Instead it was decided that I do three tasks to prove I am loyal to the Goth gang and to Snake, the first was to go into a confession box and urinate in it, the second to steal fruit from a market stall, and finally to cut my hand and share my blood with Snake. He had a thing about blood, which I never fully understood it was most strange.

My first task had to be the worst ever I entered a catholic church and the gang kept look out as I checked the door hoping it was locked and that I could be saved from the humiliation of this deed. Alas it was open and so I went in nervously and immediately dropped my knickers and urinated on the floor, it seemed to last for ages and although it was dark I swear I could see the shiny wet floor. I was soon out of there and actually saw urine coming out of the box that had to be evidence of my deed. A priest went in soon after with a catholic woman and came straight out in discussed. My second task was simple stealing fruit I took a pile of oranges off a fruit stall and ran swiftly, a man ran after me but he was too slow and I escaped unharmed. The third task was painful and bizarre as I cut my hand with a knife and Marsha was asked to cut hers, we were made to join hands and Snake captured our blood in the palm of his hand and licked it off like a vampire.

I was often curious about the plans made by Snake as he was clearly not singing from the same hymn sheet as me, he definitely had a slate missing off the roof and that concerned me greatly. I often wondered whether or not he was on medication for some sort of mental illness. Not being an expert I could not put my finger on what exactly was wrong with him. But I had joined the gang for a reason, for protection and that was my excuse for what it was worth. The weird eccentricities displayed by Snake added to an unsettled feeling that I had from the start, I suppose that I was curious to see whether or not he was truly insane or just bizarre.

We often went for night walks especially on foggy nights; we were like silhouettes in the lamp lit streets immerging like figures from time. Imagine a Dickens movie like Oliver Twist or something like Sherlock Holmes, it was as if we had entered a time warp and were living in Victorian England. Goth was cool but I felt uneasy, as we seemed to up set a lot of people with our antics. For anyone who saw us I should imagine we looked quite menacing, wearing our black attire and acting strangely.

As Goths we were devoted to our music and life style I was living with Juicy Lucy for my sins and my god I was paying dearly for that. She was one annoying bitch with her silly laugh and dozy ways it was only one step better than living with wanking Tom and tormenting Gary. What we lesbians have to put up with. Masturbation was all right but not when you got disturbed doing it, after all I once caught Tom cranking his pole and he caught me weaving the basket, so I guess we were evens. Well its normal and I bet even royalty does it at times, there must be royal tossers somewhere.

Snake suddenly spun round his long coat flowed as he did so; he had a look of devilment in his eyes.
"Let's have some fun" He announced
He looked around him and smiled "It's a perfect evening for fun"
When he acts like this you can expect problems, he was bored and needed excitement. Everyone looked to him for inspiration after all he was the dark messiah and what he said was to be happened.

Drab looked at the others with a vacant expression on his face

"Are you with us Drab?" Snake asked

"Just thinking" Drab replied

"Well don't fucking strain your head Drab" Marsha said teasing him

"Why do you keep picking on Drab?" I asked Marsha

"Keep your nose out widow" Marsha said poking me in the shoulder

I was so angry at her attitude towards me and constantly picking on Drab.

"Why what you gonna do if I don't Marsha?" I said challenging her

"Just keep on black Widow and you will see" Marsha said pointing at me

"Now girls, lets be nice ok" Snake advised

"My god Marsha what have you got against me?" I asked her in order to bring our problems out in the open.

"I don't know I just don't like you" Marsha admitted

"But we all need to get on we are like family" Snake chipped in.

"So no bitchiness he went on".

"I agree" Drab said

"You would you freak because you fancy her, but she's gay brain ache"

Marsha ought to have been called Snake as she had so much venom That was the last straw I heard her remarks towards Drab and lost my temper, I charged at Marsha and pushed her. She stepped back at the same time and landed me a cunning blow to the face. I thought my nose was going to explode as her fist made contact I fell back and Marsha saw her opportunity and jumped on top of me. Normally I would enjoy this but Marsha was one hateful lady and she had the advantage being such a crafty madam. Marsha was hitting my head on the pavement until I managed to knee her in the back, then I did what girls do best grabbed her hair and pushed her off me. I then returned a punch to the nose and a thump to the chest. We seemed to be rolling around the pavement for ages until Snake and a few others stopped us.

We both stood with blood on our faces staring at each other with hatred in our eyes. Snake was pacing up and down and so disappointed with us and the others just remained quiet. We were still being held while Snake suddenly slapped us both on the face in temper.

"This does not happen ever, you are both fucking idiots" He then noticed that he had blood from both off us on his fingers and sucked it off.

"Let's go back to the church" He insisted.

I had a nightmare that very same evening; I fell asleep and began dreaming of vampires. Snake appeared at the church and was making eyes at me; he put me in a trance and my god I was under his spell. It was horrid suddenly he had fangs and was sucking the blood from my neck. I went white and collapsed onto the church alter, where other vampires like Marsha also bit me and sucked my blood. I woke up in a cold sweat and staring into the darkness, hoping it was just a dream. It felt so real and Snake made a good vampire, his lust for blood made me think so and as for Martha well her wild behaviour was evident in my dream. I came to life as a vampire and walked through a graveyard, I travelled through mist and felt totally alone. Other vampires who floated around me in mid air, each one looked magnificent in their costumes suddenly joined me and their fangs were shining in the moonlight. A loud sound echoed in the darkness and we had vampire hunters pursuing all of us. I found it difficult to fly properly and felt something pierce my side, I fell to the ground and a ugly man held up a sharp steak to my chest. He drew back and then forced it into my chest and I awoke from the dream petrified.

I remained with the Goth gang for two years, going to the church having parties and listening to the Goth music they were happy days and I found my true identity there and then. I must say I did enjoy most of my time with them, until I reached the age of eighteen. In fact I even celebrated my eighteenth birthday with them in Gothic style. Snake remained the leader of the gang and Marsha remained by his side, but he became stranger than ever. Marsha was always jealous of Snake and I, she hated the attention that he gave me although I am a lesbian; Marsha thought I was a bi sexual. Snake also attempted to kiss me and made a fuss of me, she even heard him discussing how fed up he was with her and her clinging ways. This made Marsha more determined to get rid of me out of the gang; she never liked me and was obviously planning this for some time. We had many verbal fights but tried to keep the peace for the sake of the gang. But even some of the gang members were finding other interests and were hardly ever together. People were starting to mistrust Snake and no longer think of him as some sort of messiah, he had lost his credibility since his strange behaviour.

Marsha left the gang for a while, but returned trying to rekindle her love for Snake. But Snake still tried to come on to me and rejected her pursuits, this angered her and she continued to plan her revenge on me. Then on what I would consider the worst night of my life Marsha sat in the church beside Snake, she was looking a little sheepish with a guilty look on her face. It was as if she had done something wrong. The moon was full and Snake was particularly agitated pacing up and down in the church. I noticed someone standing near him who I had not seen before; he was wearing a leather jacket and looked unshaven with a front tooth missing. I approach them hoping to find out what was happening but they were being very secretive. I asked Clay about him but all he could give me was his name 'Weed' and that he was into drugs. I must confess drugs certainly were not my scene and I was not about to try them. So the presence of Weed didn't please me, I was contemplating leaving them at this point but Clay gave me some cider and I foolishly stayed. I was relaxed drinking my cider god knows how much I had but I felt merry and I found that even Drab was interesting to talk to. My god I felt good at this point, but I remember saying to someone that I had a headache probably due to the cider. Someone passed me some tablets and I felt as if I was flying through clouds.

I think that it must have been Marsha looking back at the turn of events. Soon after this we went out and Snake was calmer although he seemed to be on a mission, he beckoned us on into the night under the light of the full moon. Snakes eyes were red and his pupils were dilated he was acting strange, out of character even for him. I think we were all high on something I remember being confused and my body didn't seen as if it belonged to me. Fudge seemed breathless clinging hold of her fat as she walked down the street. It was like looking at a dark marsh mellow and Juicy was dancing in the street.

Suddenly we met a rival gang across the street, they were rockers dressed in leather jackets and jeans. They began taunting us shouting abuse one of the Goths shouted back abuse but added a few choice words of his own; they referred to us as weirdoes or pathetic freaks. This cause tension between both gangs and we were soon in a fight. Fists were flying, kicking and brawling in the street. This is when Marsha seized her opportunity and began kicking one of the girls in the other gang behind me. She managed to get her on the ground and continued punching and kicking her. I tried to stop her but felt something hard hitting my head and I fell to the ground dazed. Marsha saw her chance and began kicking me; it was awful I lay next to the other girl who looked badly beaten. Suddenly I heard police sirens and before long both the gangs disbursed and both the girl and I were alone. I stood up and looked at her, I wanted to help her, but I was handcuffed and she was being helped by the police an ambulance came and took her away and guess who got blamed for her beating. Yes I did, although I was dazed and confused I could beat up a girl and do such amazing things. I could feel blood on my face and my ribs felt broken as I ducked my head down in order to get into the police car. I remember hearing the girls name mentioned Joanna, so I repeated it to myself so that I wouldn't forget it. I felt so bad about her although it wasn't my fault; I suppose I should have made more effort to save her. If my head wasn't so fucked up I could have helped her, but things were so insane and those tablets were no doubt ecstasy. So I am a druggy and maybe a murderer, in a Goth gang and god knows what else I was hospitalised and then went to the police station, handcuffed and never left alone.

TRAGEDY

Following the tragic attack on the young girl Joanna who by some miracle survived, I was held in the local police station, I was sat in a cell looking at the horrid walls and iron door which I had previously seen on television in cop shows. I never thought for one moment that I would be in one, next comes the interrogation. The strong light in the face and asked to talk and reveal all, my god will I fuck. Although the heating is on it still seems freezing, colder than that church that I was in, oh to be a Goth. I still think of Mrs Cooper and being back at school those moments of being bullied and my glory day striking back. My god I defended myself that day, no fucker was going to bully me forever. You can only take so much then blow, give the bastards everything you've got, don't let them beat you.

Oh here we go the doors being unlocked and footsteps; of course it takes an army to escort me to the interrogation room, my god sad bastards. They led me to a room with a great big mirror, probably two was so they could psycho analyse me and say what a poor child led into this situation, deprived of parental love and all that bollocks. My god I do love these places, sitting on a plastic chair with a wooden table and strangers in the room. A woman say beside me and introduced herself as my legal representative called Kathy, my god she was ugly, everybody has the right to be ugly but she abused the privilege. She had obviously fell out the ugly tree and hit every branch on the way down.

One of the officers sat staring at me like I was a freak, in the end I couldn't help myself I gave him a visual sign with my index finger basically saying screw you pal. It didn't go down to well I guess he wasn't getting any from his misses and took it out on me. It was a case of good cop bad cop the policewoman was nicer and I do love a woman in uniform, they are so superior and domineering. I must confess I am a submissive lesbian who likes to be told what to do sexually. So back to the interrogation with the policeman with a big nose postman pat with an attitude. He questioned me about my actions and reminded me of my school report, the one-day that I defended myself and I get this shit. He leaned forward almost in my face I could almost lick his nose, or tickle all the strands of hair growing out of it.

"So why join a gang?" He asked

Before I had chance to answer he was in with the next question

"Is it because you thrive on beating girls up?" He said with a smirk

"No I fucking well don't I was the one being bullied at school and who helped me then? No one so I had to defend myself or continued being bullied not like you arse holes would understand that" I said in anger.

"Wow temper Jodie" He said with his hands up
Even the female officer looked at him with disgust

She cleared her throat and began talking to me softly but with authority "Jodie we realise its been difficult for you, but beating up a girl is no answer, why do that?"

"I guess I wanted to be noticed in the gang as they protected me"

I completely lost it, I was lying so the gang didn't get into trouble I was actually protecting Marsha, knowing the bitch wouldn't defend me in any way. The rest of interview went reasonably well I just kept quiet shed a few crocodile tears and then waited for the outcome. I was genuinely upset about that poor girl lying dead in the street, my tears were for her and no fucker else.

I was an hour in the interview room waiting for my parents to arrive, which was an agonising time when they came in and almost blanked me. I was clearly invisible as the police spoke to them in length about my behaviour. All I could do was sit there kicking my feet against the table with my boots on and thinking this is the first time that I have seen my parents in months. My father made an exhibition of himself saying how he had provided for the family and I was the only problem in his life, yes bull shit dad. Mother just broke down in tears and gave it the woe is me treatment. I suppose this is parenthood, not for me I am glad that I am a lesbian no kids and no hassle, apart from now of course.

The end result meant that I had to go to prison for a short time, on my fathers request he wanted me punished and was determined to let them do this. The judge said that I was to be made an example of to deter other gangs from doing the same harm to an individual. The jury sat looking at me as if I had two heads and came out of a circus, I dressed Goth so what get over it. I was going to explain that not all Goths are in gangs and fight but who would believe me, these chosen people the jury from all walks of life most of them didn't even want to be there. They didn't care about me just got their day off work and got paid for sending me down.

I still see my fathers face as he shouted send her down and punish her for what she's done and I suppose if the tables were turned I would have done the same thing. I understand that he was actually heart broken having to make that decision based on the evidence provided, I really don't blame him at all. I might even say the next years did me good because I became stronger and more determined to fight my disability called dyslexia.

I was taken to a women's open prison for six months and my god was that rough, I was stripped which was nice and searched. Then examined by a doctor for my fitness and her pleasure no doubt purvey bitch. I was then taken inside to meet other prisoners and officers, some were definitely butch lesbians and my gaydar was on checking them over.

I was assigned to a job in the prison on laundry as Chinese washerwoman calling me wha wen wong, a question I always ask myself. I visited all areas of the prison collecting washing from the beds and prisoners; I must say some bedding was disgusting. It was a case of blood, piss, other body fluids and shit, sometimes-sweaty towels and sheets. Often you could match the bedding with the prisoner just looking at each one and thinking my god I am in for a treat today. I did my time at that prison and knew about it blood sweat and years I called it, with no time off for good behaviour. Some young girls were less hard than me and got sucked into the meanest bunch of hard-core prisoners ever known; they were bait on the hook no danger.

I lay in my cell each night reflecting on my past I was a mere eighteen year old spending my time in prison bored out of my tiny head. I did wonder how that girl had been getting on that I allegedly beat up. I did feel bad that I was once being bullied and now I am classed as a bully it was not what I wanted. Now I was classed as a young offender and had a criminal record doing time in affect for Marsha.

To be honest I wanted to punish myself but I couldn't quite think of how I could do this effectively, then I cam up with a plan. If I could get someone else to do this I would be satisfied in my own mind that I was being punished and could sleep at night without having a conscience. T he way to do this was to approach the top dog and insult her, this would lead to her beating me up and therefore I was punished. This was possibly a strange way to get punished but effective if I wanted to be free from guilt.

I planted the seed by making it known that I thought Doggie was a fat tart with nothing better to do with her time than shagging fresh new girls. It worked a treat telling the right people, the gossip reached her in seconds and she was after me. I headed for the shower and one of the women alerted doggie, I was in the shower when she arrived looking angry and mean.

"Well what's this then pretty girl?" Doggie began

"Oh, hi there" I shouted bravely

"What are you staring at, do you like what you see" Doggie said posing.

"No I don't like butch women" I said looking her up and down

"What did you say Lesbo?" Doggie asked

"You heard you're too butch for me, excess fat and all that" I was shaking with fear inside as I said this.

"Hey girls why don't we teach this gay bitch a lesson?" Doggie said addressing her friends

"Perhaps she prefers me" said one of her friends covered in tattoos

"I must admit your dishy" I said admiring her tattoos

"Nah she wants it rough so lets give it her rough" Doggie said grabbing my hair and pulling her out of the shower, each girl began to slap me, but I wanted punishment not pleasure.

"Pass me that broom Debbie" Doggie said without taking her eyes off me.

She asked them to pin me down and I seriously thought she was going to insert the broom into my virginals. She held it tight and asked them to hold me still, then she stopped and laughed really loud, I was bracing myself for the worst and thought my worst nightmare was about to happen.

But she broke the stick on her knee and threw it away, then in temper she started bunching me hard in the stomach and face. Each blow was like being hit with a rock and I felt myself getting weaker and weaker until I collapsed. The floor was a mess with soap suds and my blood, I crawled to the place where I had left my clothes and tried to focus but my eye was closing. The next thing I remember was my friend jasmine helping me back to my cell. My god my face was a mess and I could hardly walk I swear I had broken ribs.

After this Doggie and every other bully targeted me I was like flavour of the month, every problem was caused by me and I was getting slapped, punched and a subject of laughter it was worse than school for a while.

But I did go mad when my friend Jasmine got beat up she was so badly injured she ended up in the prison hospital. I was so angry I went after Doggie to teach her a lesson she would never forget.

I marched towards Doggies cell her friends Sue and Debbie were there guarding the door like 10 Downing street. One of them put her arm out to stop me and found herself on thee floor in seconds holding her throat. So the other rushed forward and I drop kicked her in the stomach, then punched her in the jaw. I remember shouting or screaming like a banshee as I entered Doggies cell, she knew I meant business as she was immediately on the defensive trying to attack me with a chair.

"Now bitch it's my turn" I shouted

I ploughed into her like a bull, firstly with a high kick to the chest and then without stopping I gave her one punch after another until she went down hard onto the ground. Debbie and Sue entered the cell but kept their distance from me as they tried picking Doggie up, I watched her chest rise so that I knew she was breathing then left the cell. Two prison wardens took me to the governor's office, but I was just given a warning and extra duties. Most of the time the wardens let you fight your own battles, as it was a tussle for power and survival of the fittest that's what prison is basically all about. Reform was just a buzzword branded about by the local goodie goodies that just wanted to be seen doing something for prisoners. No one fully understood peoples past lives and what made them commit crimes, the poverty and hardships of prisoners. Parents who were alcohols or drug addict what chance had any child got growing up in that kind of environment. Doggie was brought up with a schizophrenic mother and a violent drunken father; she just knew how to be a prostitute in order to survive. Pat was brought up to steal and it became a way of life to con people, she knew no other life. I was also amazed at the amount of dyslexic prisoners all went to school but slipped through the net struggling to survive in society. Either you form your own strategies to read and write or you just give in and blame society for your lack of education or in failing to acknowledge your disability.

Education was available in prison, but it was up to the individual to seek the courses and enrol, help was out their, if you made the effort to go and find out more. I was approached after the incident with Doggie and I took it, before long I was doing O 'levels in five subjects and went on to A' levels when I left prison. Things were looking up after that day in the governor's office.

However later that day I was in the exercise yard, when Doggie approached me, she had a gang of women around her who formed around me in one big circle. A number of officers watched as Doggie moved forward towards me, no one else moved and the atmosphere was tense.

The prison wardens looked on but then appeared surprised as Doggie put out her hand in friendship. I was very surprised and put out my hand to shake hers, she held my hand firmly and smiled

"Few people have dared challenge me, no one has ever beaten me"
Doggie said humbly
I could only smile back and listen to her
"Your one fucking brave lady" Doggie looked into my eyes

"I was merely defending myself" I admitted.

"Well you can certainly fight" Doggie said admiringly

At that the crowd dispersed.

"How did you learn to fight like that?" Doggie asked

"I had a good teacher, he taught me to defend myself" I explained

"So why did you let me beat you up in the shower?" Doggie asked confused

"I needed to be punished because I fucked up being in a gang" I wanted to tell her everything and why not she was hardly going to meet Marsha.

So I told her all about the Goth gang and my circumstances and to my surprise she was so sympathetic and understanding of my situation. Her advice to me was to seek education fight dyslexia like I fought her and make peace with my parents. I swore never again to misjudge people and I would also help anyone who needed it no matter who they were. Doggie admired my artwork and made me promise not just to pursue education but also to seek a career.

As things turned out it seems that Joanna the girl I allegedly beat up explained to the police that I was innocent she was alive told the police that Marsha was the guilty one who assaulted her. So I was officially vindicated and guess who was coming to jail and doing time for her crime? It was one other than Marsha. Yes I was to be released and she was coming in and serving twelve months for that and a further time for drug dealing. I was to be released but had no idea where I was going for the next six months. My parents wanted me back but I was not prepared to go home just yet. I was given the opportunity to work in a holiday camp with good references and a clean record. That at least was a start and I could think about my future while cleaning out chalets and having fun at a major holiday camp.

Marsha appeared in the prison and at that point I was being escorted out, we passed each other and I launched at her taking everyone by surprise. Two guards pulled me off her but not until I had punch her directly in the face. She was holding her face and blood was oozing through her fingers, she looked scared and was reluctant to retaliate, I was so angry at seeing her I decided to offer her a little verbal service.

"You fucking bitch, you nearly ruined my life" I said still being held "Make her suffer girls, make her pay for what she has done".

I left the prison free and innocent of the crimes that I had been convicted for. Am I bitter, am I fuck; I just wanted to move on and do something different. I needed a further break from the parents and the holiday camp seemed like a good place to go away and rethink my life. I was now more educated and perhaps more mature; I was almost a sensible woman.

TIME OUT

I began work at the holiday camp it was nice to wake up and smell the sea. Up early with my equipment consisting of a mop, bucket and rags armed to the teeth to clean chalets. My word I was going to scrub them chalets until they gleamed I planned to be the best scrubber in the camp. By that I don't mean a tart there were enough of them about drooling after the entertainers enough to make me vomit. I was there to have some fun and seek out the odd woman or two my god some were odd too. Catering seemed to attract them as well as the entertainment department. Honestly if the entertainment held a contest for the dirtiest, scruffiest, ugliest women I new a building full of them.

The funniest image was seeing teabags being dried on the washing line, as if there was a shortage, perhaps the foreign tea merchants lost their cargo at sea. My god I wondered what else was going to hang on the line, some things were asking to be pinched. It's funny what happens at these holiday camps plenty of fun for holidaymakers and staff. But no mixing together having relationships with the punters as they are called by the staff. But we did have chalet parties and anyone was invited and virtually anything goes, or so it seems.

I worked a season in this environment and people began to realise I could sing quite well. I was singing at the karaoke night and the entertainment manager arranged for me to have a personal spot in a show and my own stage show in another theatre. But I was not the type of person who liked fame or popularity; give me the bullying any time, my god not really. It was fun while it lasted and I will treasure the memories there, but I really wanted to go home and be educated. I wanted a career in art and design, or in fashion design demonstrating my artistic flair.

COMING BACK HOME

I dreaded the moment when I had to see my parents again; I didn't know how they would respond to me, after all my father wanted me to spend time in jail and pay my debts to society as he put it (Punishment). I would love to have seen his face when he discovered that I was innocent. My god, may I say that I was getting more nervous as I got closer to the house. It was strange seeing the old curtains in the windows that I despised so much. I noticed someone peeping from behind the curtains and recognised it to be my father. Suddenly he rushed out the front door; he then stopped and stood in front of me. I looked into his eyes as he looked back at me then looked down in shame. We both stood for a while neither of us saying anything, it was one of them moments that you dread to happen. Finally he gave a cough in order to clear his throat and spoke to me with tears in his eyes.

"I am so sorry Jodie, I feel as if I have let you down" He said his voice was quivering

"Dad I am sorry too, for putting you through absolute hell" I said sorrowfully

At that we embraced and the tears poured like a waterfall, we were observed by the rest of the family who had congregated around the door.

And my god, the entire neighbourhood god bless the sad bastards who looked on at our reconciliation.

Well, what can I say about the things that followed on, my education at university and my career as a designer. Things finally worked out for the better my parents never seized to bang on about being proud of me and my education. Same old shit really for years after and well I came through, I could be a good example for others, maybe even a role model but hey I did what was right. I had some flack on the way but I made it and now wear the t-shirt to prove it.

I often wondered what happened to Snake and the other guys from my Goth period apparently Snake was a manic depressive (by polar) which explained his mania at times and depression which were considered his mood swings. Snake was reported to have died by committing suicide taking his life by jumping off a railway bridge. I still dress as I please in Goth style but no one bothers me these days I am still me Jodie, the individual with my own style and personality.

The rest of the gang had dispersed after my jail sentence and all gone their separate ways. No one really kept in touch, but I do know that Marsha was released from prison and met someone moved away from the area got in touch with a mutual friend and oh my god actually asked about me. She now has two children and wanted to apologise for her behaviour to me.

Doggie continued to commit crimes and will probably never change I wrote to her at her favourite place her majesty's pleasure or prison. I explained about my graduation and thanked her for her support god bless Doggie me touch mate. I did get some sort of scribbled letter as a reply that said thank you for bringing me back to reality or life in the real world love from Doggie.

My life had changed and I had grown up I attended university and graduated from their and became a top designer of fashion. Sometimes you have to go through the rough to reach the smooth. My parents discovered this but my god they still invite those peculiar guests will they never learn. Even though I changed I still support those individuals who want to be different, we all need identity and a place in life without being ridiculed or hated for it. My advice to you is to be yourself and no one else, follow your own thoughts, dreams and desires as long as they hurt no one else. And like I say I will always be Jodie the individual dressed how I want and pleasing me as a person.

Remember to donate to the Sophie Lancaster foundation online https://www.sophielancasterfoundation.com

INFLUENTIAL GOTHIC SONGS

I walk the line- Alien sex fiend

Yumma yumma man- Daniella Dax

Were so happy – The dawn society

SOME OF MY OTHER BOOKS